# Clifford's™ puppy days

# LOTS OF LOVE

by Sarah Fisch

Illustrated by Jay Johnson

Based on the Scholastic book series
"Clifford The Big Red Dog"
by Norman Bridwell

No part of this publication may be reproduced in whole or in part, stored in a retrieval system, or transmitted in any form or by any means, electronic, mechanical, photocopying, recording, or otherwise, without written permission of the publisher. For information regarding permission, write to Scholastic Inc., Attention: Permissions Department, 557 Broadway, New York, NY 10012.

ISBN-13: 978-0-545-02843-1
ISBN-10: 0-545-02843-4

Designed by Michael Massen

12  11  10  9  8  7  6  5                    10 11 12 13 14 15/0

Printed in the U.S.A.        40
First printing, February 2008

## SCHOLASTIC INC.

New York     Toronto     London     Auckland     Sydney
Mexico City     New Delhi     Hong Kong     Buenos Aires

February is a cold winter month.

"*Brr!* No wonder it only has twenty-eight days," said Emily Elizabeth's father.

"Valentine's Day is coming, though,"
Emily Elizabeth said. "We have lots of
love to give, don't we, Clifford?"

Emily Elizabeth had been thinking about all the dogs in the city without homes. "Valentine's Day is the perfect day to visit a dog shelter!" Emily Elizabeth said.

The next day, Emily Elizabeth woke
Clifford up early. "Today's a special day!"
she told the tiny red puppy.

Clifford, Emily Elizabeth, and Mrs. Howard
walked to a red brick building.

"'Love For Paws,'" Emily Elizabeth read.
"This is it!"

"Hi!" said a smiling young man.
"Welcome to Love For Paws!
My name is Alex."

"Hi, Alex," said Emily Elizabeth. "We brought valentine treats and toys for all the dogs!"

"Great!" said Alex. "Let me show you around."

"This is our kennel area," said Alex.

Clifford saw a long hallway of cages.

There were big dogs, little dogs, dogs with

short hair, and dogs with long hair.

Some dogs barked, and all of them wagged their tails.

"How did all these dogs get here?" asked Emily Elizabeth.

"Some were left here by people who couldn't take care of them," Alex said. "We rescued others from the street."

Alex said, "We take good care of them, but they all need a good home and someone to love them."

"What happens if they don't find
homes?" asked Mrs. Howard.

"The dogs can live here as long as it
takes," answered Alex.

"Sarge has lived here for three years. I
hope somebody special will take him home
one day."

"Hi, Sarge," Clifford barked.

"Hi there, kiddo," the old dog said in a gruff voice. "Nice family you got there."

"Thanks," Clifford said. He felt very lucky.

Next Alex took them to the veterinarian.
He took care of dogs who were sick or
injured.

"Hey, Dr. Dwyer!" Alex said. "These folks are volunteering today."

"What a great way to spend Valentine's Day!" said Dr. Dwyer.

"This is our play yard," Alex said.

"All the dogs get to exercise and play

outside every day."

Clifford had never seen so many dogs.

"Hi!" barked a puppy almost as tiny as
ord. "I'm Toby! Have you come to live
oo?"

"I'm Clifford," said the tiny red puppy.
"I'm just visiting."

"Oh well," Toby said. "Wanna play chase?"

"Sure!" Clifford barked. "I'm It!"

A smiling little old man with a gray
mustache walked up to Alex.

"I'm Mr. Morgan," he said.

"I'd like to adopt a dog, but I think these puppies are too young for a man my age." He laughed. "Do you have older dogs?"

Clifford liked Mr. Morgan's friendly
smile and gray mustache.

It reminded him of someone he just met!
He barked and barked.

Alex laughed. "I think I know what you're thinking," he said. "Come with me, Mr. Morgan."

"This is Sarge," said Alex.

"Isn't he great?" Emily Elizabeth said.

"Oh my goodness," gasped Mr. Morgan. "He is certainly very handsome! Would you like to come home with me, Sarge?"

Sarge barked happily.

Sarge had found a friend for life.

"He's my kind of guy, Clifford!" Sarge
said. "At last, I'm going home!"

Emily Elizabeth wished they could find good homes for all the dogs.

"We could come back and volunteer again," said Mrs. Howard. "We seemed to bring Sarge some luck, didn't we?"

"Yeah!" Emily Elizabeth shouted.

So Emily Elizabeth and Mrs. Howard
decided to visit their friends at the shelter
once a week.

Clifford thought it was a great idea!

*Valentine's Day is great,* Clifford thought.

*But dogs need love every day!*

# Do You Remember?

**Circle the right answer.**

1. Which holiday did Clifford celebrate at the dog shelter?
   a. Halloween
   b. Thanksgiving
   c. Valentine's Day

2. Which dog went home with Mr. Morgan?
   a. Toby
   b. Sarge
   c. Clifford

**Which happened first?**

**Which happened next?**

**Which happened last?**

**Write a 1, 2, or 3 in the space after each sentence.**

Clifford played chase with Toby in the play yard. \_\_\_\_\_

Clifford met Sarge in the kennel. \_\_\_\_\_

Mr. Morgan decided to adopt Sarge. \_\_\_\_\_

**Answers:**